FEB 1 4 2013

P9-CMT-153

Salvage
and
Demolition

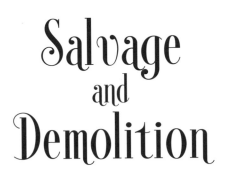

Salvage
and
Demolition

Tim Powers

Illustrated by J. K. Potter

Subterranean Press 2013

First Edition

ISBN
978-1-59606-515-4

Subterranean Press
PO Box 190106
Burton, MI 48519

www.subterraneanpress.com

To Rodger Turner
with gratitude

I

THE LAST OF the three boxes just seemed to contain litter—a dozen cigarette-butts and a dusting of ash scattered across the middle-pages of an old issue of the *San Francisco Chronicle* and a 1957 copy of *TV Guide* with a very youthful-looking Pat Boone on the cover.

Blanzac sat back, tapping the ash off his own cigarette onto the old carpet under his chair, and took off his reading glasses to peer past the narrow glow of the desk lamp

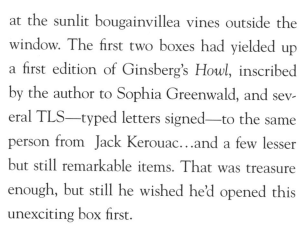

at the sunlit bougainvillea vines outside the window. The first two boxes had yielded up a first edition of Ginsberg's *Howl*, inscribed by the author to Sophia Greenwald, and several TLS—typed letters signed—to the same person from Jack Kerouac...and a few lesser but still remarkable items. That was treasure enough, but still he wished he'd opened this unexciting box first.

He sighed and slid his glasses on again, and lifted out the *TV Guide* and the newspaper, and then his hopes brightened again. Under an old science fiction paperback below them lay a disordered stack of handwritten manuscript.

There was no name or title on the top sheet, and the handwriting looked feminine to him. Perhaps it was something of Sophia Greenwald's—he seemed to remember that she had been a minor poet in San Francisco in the '50s, though her niece, who had given him the boxes on consignment, had seemed unaware of that and he hadn't mentioned the vague recollection to her. Were there any Sophia Greenwald collectors?

He turned to his computer and called up the Google screen and typed in her name. According to Wikipedia she'd been born in 1926, lived in San Francisco, had two books of poetry published, in 1953 and 1955, left San Francisco in 1957 and died of cholera in Mexico in 1969 at the age of forty-three.

He picked up the top sheets of the manuscript. It did appear to be poetry—many of the lines ended well short of the right-hand edge of the paper.

He puzzled out a few lines from the middle of the page—

...And, slick with juice, it slipped, but quick his hand
Caught firm a hold, and brought it to his face—
To hesitate a heartbeat—God's command
Still seemed to echo in this sylvan place;

And Adam saw before him stretch two lives:
One to move in God's shadow, acquiesce
In all responses, reflexes and drives;
The other...ah, the other! To express
His own will, print himself upon this world!
He chose—and bit—and dimmed each future dawn—
As helplessly as shadows fall unfurled
To west instead of east as dusk come on,
As fated as the phases of the moon...

He read through several pages of it, pausing sometimes to puzzle out a word, and the narrative gradually shifted from a distorted re-telling of Genesis to an oddly compelling view of the old Ptolemaic earth-centered universe, with the sun and planets fixed on crystal spheres that spun like clockwork inside a vast ultimate sphere... then the focus returned to Adam and Eve and Cain and Abel, and their vividly detailed sacrifices and crimes were made to seem as mechanical as the motions of the spheres.

He forgot about the other items in the boxes, absorbed in the fluid narrative of the poem, but after a few minutes he jumped at a cold tap on the back of his neck, and then drops of water were pattering on his desk.

He lunged out of his chair and spread his corduroy jacket to cover the Kerouac letters and the Ginsberg book, and as he cursed and fumbled them into the last box and hugged it against his shirt he squinted over his shoulder, certain that the window was open and a sprinkler had come on—

But even before he snatched off his glasses to see clearly across the room, he was aware of the dry-white-wine smell of rain on pavement, and a whiff of chocolate; and he caught a familiar melody, and a hissing like tires on a wet street, growing more audible and then fading.

A moment later the falling water had stopped, the music was gone, and the room once again smelled only of cigarette smoke and coffee and old book paper.

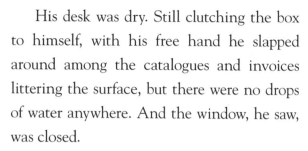

His desk was dry. Still clutching the box to himself, with his free hand he slapped around among the catalogues and invoices littering the surface, but there were no drops of water anywhere. And the window, he saw, was closed.

He glanced up—the ceiling was dry and uncracked.

He sat down and carefully slid the box back onto the desk, but for several seconds he simply stared at it and took reassurance from breathing in and out. The flaps of the box had sprung open, and he could see that the books and papers in it were perfectly dry.

The brief moment of impossible rain had apparently never happened.

At last he sighed deeply and sat back in his chair.

You had a hallucination, he told himself cautiously, but it's over. Probably you shouldn't open the Wild Turkey bottle before noon anymore; this was a warning, I'll cut back, no problem. I'm glad the books and letters didn't actually get wet!

It was late afternoon now, though, so he let himself reach out, a bit shakily, and pick up his glass. He wasn't aware of the rigidity of his neck until the resonant warmth of the swallowed bourbon loosened his muscles.

The hallucinated melody, he realized belatedly, had been "How Little We Know." Long time since I heard that one, he thought.

Then his face went cold again, for his gaze had fallen on the science fiction paperback, and, though he hadn't given it more than a glance a few moments earlier, he was sure that it was now a different book; its cover had been dark purple, some kind of outer space scene with planets or rockets or something of that sort, but now it was green and yellow—giant lizards chasing men in a jungle with *What Vast Image* in lurid lettering across the top.

He put down his glass and picked up the book, hoping that it would somehow look

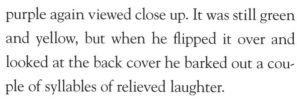

purple again viewed close up. It was still green and yellow, but when he flipped it over and looked at the back cover he barked out a couple of syllables of relieved laughter.

It was two books bound together *tête-bêche,* back to back, one upside-down to the other, and the reverse cover was the remembered purple one, titled, he saw, *Seconds of Arc.* The author of both was Daniel Gropeshaw, a name Blanzac didn't recognize. Now he noticed the blue band at the top of each cover: ACE DOUBLE NOVEL BOOKS TWO COMPLETE NOVELS, and he recalled that William Burroughs' first book had been published by Ace Books as one half of a similar pair.

He looked at both title pages, but neither was signed, and he tossed it onto the desk. A moment later the telephone rang.

He cleared his throat and hummed a few notes of "How Little We Know" to be sure his voice wouldn't come out shrill, then picked up the receiver and said, "Hello?"

"Richard Blanzac? I'm Amy Mathis with Goldengrove Retirement Community, in Oakland, and one of our residents asked us to call you. Her name is Betty Barlow, Elizabeth Barlow, and she wishes to talk to you about… some books, she said."

"Books?" Blanzac was still blinking doubtfully at the desk and the closed window and the dry, unblemished ceiling. "Books, you say. To sell?"

"Some books you have, I gathered."

"She wants to what, buy some?"

A sigh came down the line. "That might be. She asked that you visit her here. I gather from your area code that you're in the Bay Area?"

"Yes, in Daly City, but…" He forced himself to pay attention. "Retirement community, was it? How old is she?"

A bit snippily, the woman replied, "She's entirely alert and competent to handle her affairs, sir."

"Can I talk to her, ask what this is about?"

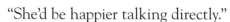

"She'd be happier talking directly."

He sighed, and was about to recommend that the old lady contact him through the mail, but the narrow office he'd made in the spare bedroom of his house suddenly seemed oppressive, even threatening. He glanced again at the window and the ceiling, and impulsively said, "What's your address?"

Goldengrove was a tranquil collage of green lawns and patios and winding brick walkways around a tan Romanesque tower and a long structure that looked like a new apartment complex. Regularly spaced cypress trees stood up behind the building, swaying against the blue late-afternoon sky.

The lobby was in the central tower, and the cathedral-high ceiling and the elegant Chippendale-style furniture made him wish he had put on a tie and a newer jacket. But the young lady at the receptionist desk cheerfully copied his name from his driver's license and directed him down one of the carpeted halls. The place smelled of violet air-freshener and rubbing alcohol.

Betty Barlow's door was open; the doorway was easily four feet wide, and Blanzac wasn't surprised to see a motorized wheelchair and an aluminum walker parked against the wall below the window, beside some rounded metal apparatus that might have been a humidifier. The blinds were open, and several frail old men in shorts and T-shirts were slumped in white plastic chairs on a patio out there.

The woman in the bed blinked at him through thick bifocals from under a thin haze of curly white hair. Her narrow body lay so straight under the smooth blanket that Blanzac thought the bed couldn't really be said to be unmade.

"Betty—Elizabeth Barlow?" he said, standing in the doorway. "I was told you want to see me."

"You're Richard Blanzac?" she said, her voice high and scratchy. When he assented, she said, "Sit down here. Those are my books you've got, you can't have them."

He moved a recent issue of *Time* magazine and a bottle of Tabasco from a nearby chair, and set them beside a telephone on a wheeled formica table by the bed. He noticed a big magnifying glass lying next to the telephone.

Barlow nodded at the Tabasco. "I go through a bottle of that a week," she said. "The food here is so bland you can't tell the puree beef from the flan. I'm the literary executor for the Sophia Greenwald estate. Have been since she died in '69." From under the blankets she produced a manila envelope. "This was in the safe, but I made them bring it to me after I got the call from Greenwald's idiot niece. Edith."

Edith Tillard was the name of the woman who had given Blanzac the three boxes of books on consignment.

The old woman reached up above her head and switched on a bright reading lamp, then picked up the magnifying glass as she slid a sheaf of folded documents out of the envelope. She riffled through them, peering at them through the glass, then handed several sheets to Blanzac.

They were a death certificate for Sophia Greenwald from a town in Mexico called Otatoclan, and letters of administration from a court in Texas, all dated in 1969. Elizabeth Barlow was indeed named executor of the Greenwald estate.

"You have a young voice," Barlow said. "How old are you?"

"I'm forty, ma'am."

"I've been executor of her estate longer than you've been alive."

Blanzac shifted uncomfortably and handed the papers back to her. "I got the books on consignment from her niece, her heir."

"You smell like cigarettes. Let me have one."

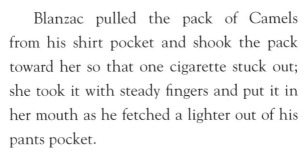

Blanzac pulled the pack of Camels from his shirt pocket and shook the pack toward her so that one cigarette stuck out; she took it with steady fingers and put it in her mouth as he fetched a lighter out of his pants pocket.

From behind him a woman's voice said, "And how are we—ah! Miss Barlow, you know there's no smoking in the building."

Blanzac turned and saw a woman in a nurse-like uniform staring past him.

"And if I get myself together to go outside," said Barlow bitterly, "those old breadsticks cough and wave their hands, even if I'm a dozen yards downwind." But she handed the cigarette back to Blanzac, who tucked it back into the pack.

Barlow glared at the woman until she retreated into the hallway, then turned to Blanzac. "Sometimes I suffer from what these people like to call dementia. You could more accurately call it something like religious ecstasy, though it does make me self-destructive sometimes. Self-destructive," she repeated, nodding. "Boxes, was it?"

"Boxes?"

"The books, Murgatroyd, the books! Ginsberg, Kerouac, Rexroth? I made some calls after idiot Edith called me—I shouldn't have."

"You called me," he said.

"I didn't call you, I had the receptionist call you." She waved at the telephone on the wheeled table. "I shouldn't have called anyone from this phone. It's in my name. The books Edith gave you are mine, you're not to touch them." She blinked at him. "Have you?"

"I've looked through Miss Tillard's boxes," he said. "Books, mainly, the 1950s San Francisco poets, as you say."

"Mainly?"

Blanzac took a deep breath. "There's what appears to be a substantial stack of autograph manuscript, as well, which might be Greenwald's work—I can give you a photocopy of it. As literary executor, you should have the text."

For several seconds she said nothing. Then, "A *manuscript!*" Her voice was hoarse. "What sort of manuscript?"

"Poetry, iambic pentameter—it looks like a hundred pages or so."

Barlow had closed her eyes, and was breathing in short gasps.

Alarmed, Blanzac started up from his chair, but she opened her eyes and stared at him. "Burn the manuscript," she whispered; then went on more loudly, "I'm her executor, you saw that. I have the authority to order you to destroy it. I—was with Sophia Greenwald when she died, and her last words were…burn that manuscript!"

"You don't know what it is!" protested Blanzac. "I don't either. It might be anything—!"

"What else was in *that* box, with the manuscript?"

Blanzac exhaled and spread his hands. "An old newspaper. A science fiction paperback. A lot of cigarette butts."

"Ach, burn the paperback too. I can compel this, legally. You don't want a lawsuit. And you must give me the books, the Ginsbergs and Rexroths, all of them."

Those belong to the niece, Blanzac thought; but let's not get into a fight about that right now. "This manuscript—you seem to know what it is. Is it something by Sophia Greenwald?"

"What if it is? She was a worthless poet. Michael McClure and Gary Snyder both said she was no good. Her books have been out of print ever since she wasn't around to boost them anymore."

He shook his head, baffled. "You're her literary executor? Wouldn't it be—"

"She made a mistake when she chose me as executor. I despise her work. For a few years I had to turn down requests to print her stuff, but—hah!— it's been decades now since anybody's even asked."

She closed her eyes, and tears were running down her wrinkled cheeks now. "Damn her vanity! Why didn't she—I can't know if you've destroyed it—even if you bring it here and burn it out on the patio where I can see, I can't know you haven't made a Xerox of it!"

And I would, thought Blanzac.

"I'll buy it," she said finally. "The manuscript and the paperback book. Calculate a fair price. And I'll have to trust your professional ethics not to make a copy before you sell it to me—part of what I'll be paying for is exclusivity. Is that acceptable, can you assure me of that condition?"

Blanzac paused before agreeing, to make it seem that he was seriously considering the terms.

Barlow went on, "Do you *care* about Sophia Greenwald's poetry? Are you a big fan?"

He smiled. "I've never read any of her work."

"It's rubbish, completely forgotten."

Forgotten because you've kept it out of print, Blanzac thought. He leaned back and crossed his arms. "Very well," he said. "Exclusivity."

"How much will it cost me?"

"I haven't even looked at it yet! How can I—"

"Give me your price, Murgatroyd," she said scornfully.

"Oh hell." The Ginsberg *Howl* would probably bring in five thousand dollars, and each of the Kerouac letters would probably do the same or better, and there were a dozen other worthwhile books in the lot. "A hundred dollars, and I sell the rest of the stuff for the niece."

The old woman scowled fiercely at him, her mouth pinched. At last she said, "And I get the science fiction paperback too."

"I'll throw that in free." And I *will* photocopy the Greenwald manuscript, he thought. After you're dead, I'll see what I can do with that.

"Go now. And talk to me here, don't call me on the telephone."

Blanzac got to his feet. "I'm sorry if I—"

She waved him away. "Get out of my sight, small-fry."

As Blanzac was walking through the Goldengrove lobby toward the front doors, squinting as he passed through horizontal bars of sunlight from the high western windows, a portly man in a wide-lapelled business suit rose from one of the Chippendale chairs and stepped in front of him. He was older than Blanzac, though he didn't look old enough to be a resident here.

"Is it Mr. Blanzac?" The man was smiling and rocking on his heels. "I hoped I'd catch you. I'm Jesse Welch, from the University of California Special Collections, and I gather you've come into possession of some literary items that concern Sophia Greenwald?"

Blanzac looked past the man toward the parking lot, then back toward the receptionist's desk.

"How did you know I'd be here?" he asked.

"She's not herself these days. What's the nature of these items?"

"Some books on consigment," said Blanzac after a moment's pause, "that belonged to Sophia Greenwald. I gather Miss Barlow is the literary executor of the Greenwald estate."

"Just books? No letters, papers?" His smile disappeared, and he was now frowning and nodding. "Miss Barlow has some unreasoning old grudge against Greenwald, and opposes any suggestion that Greenwald's work receive scholarly attention. Did the consignment include any manuscripts that might be Greenwald's?" He stared at Blanzac. "I'd see that you were well paid for turning any such over to me."

The man's insistence was a curious new factor, and Blanzac was suddenly cautious. "I've only glanced at the boxes," he said, shrugging and hoping he sounded casual. "It seems to be all books. No…papers."

"I could help you inventory the material."

"I won't be able to get to it right away. Do you have a business card? I could call you when I'm ready."

"Certainly. And could I have one of yours?"

Blanzac pulled out his wallet, pinched up one of his *Blanzac Rare Books* cards, and exchanged it with the card Welch handed him, which did appear to be genuine.

"I'll call you if I don't hear from you," said Welch.

Blanzac nodded, opened his mouth as if to say something more, then just nodded again and walked past the man, toward the doors to the parking lot. But Welch's face had seemed remotely familiar.

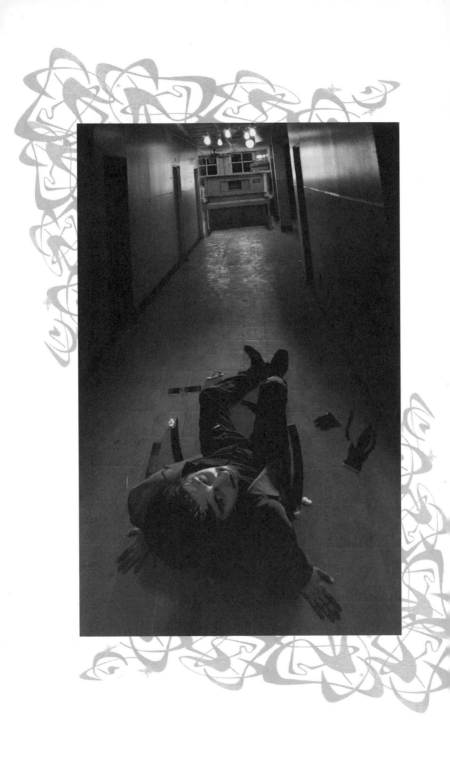

II

BACK IN HIS spare-bedroom office, Blanzac peered suspiciously at the window and the ceiling, then, reassured, allowed himself another splash of Wild Turkey as he sat down at his desk.

He took a sip of the lukewarm bourbon and then opened the third box and carefully lifted out the book and letters he had tossed into it during his hallucination an hour ago, and set them aside. It was the contested manuscript that interested him now.

He carefully gathered it up, nudged the box aside and set the stack of papers down on a clear spot on the desk, and riffled through the age-tanned pages.

The top twenty or so pages were handwritten verse, and he had read most of those earlier; below that were carbon copies of typescript. The carbons were easier to read than the inked pages had been, but after scanning a couple of lines—

Two Streams: one flowing South, the other North,

    As if from mirror'd Springs they issu'd forth

—he returned his attention to the top pages, which at least were in relatively modern English. What the hell sort of poet had Greenwald been, anyway? What he had read was hardly in any "1950s Beat poets" style. That Welch guy, impostor or not, had seemed to be familiar with her work.

Blanzac shifted in his chair to pull out his wallet, and he laid it on the desk and shuffled

through the cards till he found the one Welch had given him. Welch hadn't explained how he had come to be at Goldengrove, and he'd been awfully pushy, even for a scholar. It should be easy enough to call some central office of the University of California and verify that he was what he claimed to be.

Blanzac pulled a cigarette out of the pack in his shirt pocket and tucked it between his lips, then groped around for a lighter.

There wasn't one on the desk, and he hiked his chair around to face the nearest bookshelves.

But the bookshelves weren't there—

He had an astonished moment of looking instead down a grubby white-painted hallway with an upright piano at the far end of it, and then he had sat down hard on a linoleum floor as pieces of wood clattered around him.

He gasped, and caught the smells of Beef Stroganoff and cigarette smoke on the warm air, and from behind him shivered the babble of a lot of people talking.

He scrambled to his feet, panting and looking around wildly. In front of him was a door with a wooden *Men* sign on it, and now an unsteady young man in horn-rimmed glasses and a white shirt and striped tie came shuffling down the hall from the direction of the crowd noise. The young man kicked a piece of wood aside before lurching into the men's room, and Blanzac looked down.

He recognized the seat and disattached arms of his office chair, and there were some rectangular scraps of paper and cloth, too. He looked more closely and saw that one of them was the shaved-off spine of a first edition of *For Whom the Bell Tolls*, alongside the spine of the dust-jacket. The young man in the men's room had stepped on the cigarette Blanzac had had in his mouth.

Blanzac crouched and picked up one arm of his chair; he turned it in his shaking hands, noting the smooth, faintly-concave cut, and on an impulse he lifted it and bit it. He tasted varnish and wood.

He tossed it aside, then rubbed his palm down the painted wall, noting the coolness and the slightly gritty texture.

This could not be a hallucination.

Alcoholic blackout, he thought, almost eagerly. That's not too bad, lots of people have those. Wherever this is, you must have walked into this place, probably with someone, and now you've forgotten the past few hours. You can walk back out into the—restaurant, apparently—and fit yourself into whatever's going on, and probably figure out who you're with and bluff your way through a conversation until it all comes back to you—

Then his chest went cold and he looked down again. The wood pieces and strips of book-spine still lay on the linoleum floor.

Obviously he had not broken up his chair and torn the spine from a book and then chosen to bring the pieces along on a dinner date.

And he noticed his trousers, and then held his arms up to look at his jacket and shirt-cuffs.

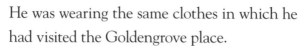

He was wearing the same clothes in which he had visited the Goldengrove place.

His fingertips were tingling and, though he had been panting a moment before, he was suddenly unable to take a deep breath.

There's a crowd, he thought. I can mix in a crowd and seem normal and inconspicuous while I…figure this out.

His pulse was pounding in his wrists and temples, but he walked steadily enough down the hall toward the rattle of cutlery and conversation. He tried to catch words or phrases, afraid that they might not be in English.

But as soon as he stepped out into the long, high-ceilinged room at the end of the corridor, a woman grabbed his elbow.

"Wow," she said, speaking loudly to be heard over the conversations at the crowded tables, "you're good!" She was looking in evident wonderment from the hall behind him to the other end of the room and back. "Even if there's a back door there by the restrooms, I don't see how you could have run around to there so quick!" Her breath smelled of gin.

Blanzac glanced down at her. She looked to be in her early thirties, a narrow pale face squinting up at him from under dark bangs and dark eyebrows, and she was wearing a black dress that seemed too big for her. Blanzac looked out across the noisy crowd, and every man he could see was wearing a sport coat and tie.

"I've got to say it's good to see you again," the woman said wryly. "But of course you're the *other* one now, the *previous* one, and you don't know who I am. Right? Hah!" She pulled him out across the floor, her black pumps knocking awkwardly on the wood. "I hope nobody took our table," she said over her shoulder.

The room was lit by white globe lamps hung from the ceiling, and Blanzac glimpsed a painted menu on the wall to his right through the layers of cigarette smoke.

She sat down at a table with two drinks and an ashtray on it and waved him to the other chair. Blanzac joined her and tried to hide the eagerness with which he picked up the drink in front of him. It proved to be bourbon, and he took a deep gulp.

"I can see for myself later," she said, "but you do have a scar in your groin from a hernia operation, right? Looks like this," she added, drawing a squiggle in the air.

"Well," he said, and the heat in his face might simply have been from the alcohol, "well, yes." Quickly he went on, "Uh, what's the name of this place again?"

"It's the Tin Angel, but you supposedly have no idea where you are. But I do *not* believe you're from the year 2012."

Blanzac swallowed the rest of his drink and exhaled. "What year," he asked carefully, "do you think it is?"

"This is 1957," she said patiently. "You said 2012 was pretty much the same, except everybody has little computers that nobody does math on, but I *know* they'll have flying cars and colonies on the moon by then."

"1957." He looked around at the room again. This could hardly be a California restaurant, with everyone smoking. Well no, it might be some sort of private club. "And we're...where?"

"The Embarcadero. San Francisco." She frowned speculatively at him. "You said you were pretty scared, right now. Are you pretty scared?"

He began laughing, and he made himself stop. "I think that's what it is," he agreed dizzily. He still didn't seem to be able to take a deep breath. "You said I'm the other one. The previous one. What...how does one get another drink? What did you mean by that?"

"The fellow who just left, who looks just like you but his clothes were damp, this afternoon he told me you'd be showing up in that hallway tonight. He remembered showing up there himself, on this night." She shook her head, not smiling now. "I'll get more drinks.

I'm scared too. Same again? It's on me, I know you don't have any money."

He touched his back pocket and realized that she was right—his wallet was still on his desk in his office. "Yes, please."

She got up and sidled her way toward the bar, and Blanzac slumped in his chair and took sidelong glances at the people at the tables around him. The men all had fairly short haircuts, nothing unusual; many of the women wore more make-up than Blanzac would have expected, but that didn't prove anything. It was certainly odd, though, that just about everybody he could see was smoking a cigarette!

He got up and crossed to a table that was not next to his own. "Excuse me," he said to the couple sitting there, "maybe you could settle a bet. Who is currently President of the United States?"

The man gave Blanzac an unfriendly look, possibly because of his open shirt and jeans. "Eisenhower," he said, emphasizing each syllable.

Blanzac nodded and went back to his own table.

Why, he asked himself, would I have come to this place? Well, I didn't come here, I fell here out of my office chair, taking pieces of it with me. But *whatever that was*, this is obviously one of those retro theme clubs, and my…date? I don't even know her name!…is playing along with the pretence; so is that Eisenhower guy. No wonder they all smoke— it's a '50s cliché, part of the costume.

The woman came shuffling back with two filled glasses, and when she had set them down beside the ashtray she looked around at the nearby tables.

"So did you ask somebody?" she said, pulling her chair out and sitting down. "I guess I shouldn't prompt you, if you haven't yet."

"You know what I asked him?"

"Who's President. He said Eisenhower. You told me half an hour ago that you did that. How fast can you drink that?"

Blanzac considered it. "Pretty fast."

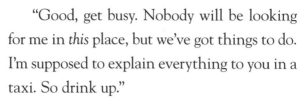

"Good, get busy. Nobody will be looking for me in *this* place, but we've got things to do. I'm supposed to explain everything to you in a taxi. So drink up."

Blanzac downed half of his drink and then hastily set it down to catch is breath.

"Who," he said hoarsely, "are you?"

She rolled her eyes. "You knew all about me when we met this afternoon—and now after all that you *really* don't know me at all?" Her expression was rueful. "I'm Sophie Greenwald. I write poetry, or I have done that, at least, and I—do translation now, for rent money. I want to quit that." She shivered and for a moment looked like a scared twelve-year-old.

Blanzac didn't move, but looked at her carefully—her wide mouth, brown eyes — and wished he had seen a picture of the real Sophia Greenwald.

Her drink was clear, with a lime slice sitting on the ice cubes, possibly a gin and tonic, and she picked it up in both hands and took a long sip of it. "And you," she said, "are Richard

Vader, you're in salvage and demolition work, whatever that is, you're forty years old, unmarried though two years ago you nearly married that horrible Gillian woman who went to work for Tiny Softs, which makes those little computers."

"Microsoft," said Blanzac faintly. It was true about Gillian—but salvage and demolition? And *Vader*? As in Darth?

"And, oh, you majored in English at City College of San Francisco, and, and—and you like the British mystery writer Ian Fleming and you don't like back rubs." She laughed and added, "And you worked for a while at a tobacco shop where the boss's name was Ted! I didn't forget!"

This was all true. Blanzac stood up, wishing he hadn't gulped the bourbon. "Let's get outside."

She tilted up her glass, then set it down empty, whistled, and got to her feet.

As they made their zig-zag way through the tables toward the front door, Blanzac's

hands were trembling and he paid particular attention to moving his legs, for he was afraid his knees might buckle. He saw many matchbooks and cigarette lighters on the tables and in people's hands, but the lighters were all metal, he saw no plastic Bics at all.

A gust of chilly sea air ruffled his hair when the woman who claimed to be Sophia Greenwald pushed open the door, and the yellow glow of streetlights gleamed on the wet, dark lanes of a highway beyond. Ragged clouds half-hid the moon in the black sky.

"I'm glad the rain finally stopped," said Greenwald. She raised one hand and stepped to the curb, looking toward the oncoming headlights. Blanzac walked up beside her— slowly, for he was watching the cars that swept past. The cars were the boxy, bulbous Chevys and Fords and Studebakers of the 1950s.

Out past the lanes of the highway and a low warehouse he could see a couple of piers and the masts of moored boats, and the patchily moonlit ocean.

"What's this street?" he asked.

"This is the Embarcadero." She turned and pointed at the street on the far side of the building and added, "That's Greenwich, and Filbert's behind us."

Blanzac frowned in puzzlement, then sprinted to the corner. The street sign over his head said Greenwich, and when he walked out to the center of the street and looked inland, he saw a steeply ascending slope of lights in the windows of bay-fronted buildings, and at the top of the hill the silhouette of Coit Tower.

He trudged back to where Greenwald was waving at an approaching taxi.

"Greenwich doesn't connect to the Embarcadero," he said. He took a deep breath. "Anymore. All this," he added as he waved around at the street and the neon Tin Angel sign over the doors behind them, "got torn out when they built the Embarcadero Freeway."

"I'd rather they'd build a spaceport," she said. The taxi, a green Chrysler that Blanzac thought looked like a big toaster, had swerved in to the curb, and Greenwald pulled open the back door and gave the driver an address on Divisadero Street, then folded herself onto the rear seat and moved over to make room for Blanzac. And when he had got in too and pulled the door shut, she slid the plexiglass partition closed.

She raised her hands, then let them drop in her lap as the cab accelerated away from the curb. "Earlier today you told me what I'm going to say to you now. You said it was disjointed. I work for a group of scholars, or something—"

"God!" The cab had turned right on Pacific Avenue, and though Blanzac vaguely recognized the buildings they were passing, the Transamerica pyramid no longer reared its tapering forty-eight stories above the rooftops to his left. "I'm sorry, go on—uh, scholars. In goddamn *1957!*"

"What, you think we're all dumb, way back here in the past?"

"No, I'm just beginning to believe it really *is* 1957." He gripped his elbows and rocked back and forth on the seat.

She gave him a puzzled look in the dimness. "*I'm* actually beginning to believe you really *are* from 2012," she said, almost to herself. She reached across the seat and thoughtfully rubbed a pinch of his jacket between her thumb and forefinger. "But yes," she went on briskly, dropping her hand, "scholars. They've hired me to translate parts of a very old Sumerian text, and I'm probably the only person alive qualified to do it, but—but I want to quit, and they don't want to let me." She shook her head. "Damn it, when I met you on North Point today you already *knew* all this!"

Blanzac shrugged, only half listening to her. Am I here, now, forever? he wondered. I *think* she's saying that I'm soon to jump from this night back to an earlier point in this day. After that, do I stay here? My God, Hemingway and Faulkner are still alive! I bet signed first editions of things like *Three Stories*

and Ten Poems and *The Marble Faun* are under a hundred bucks!

She was staring at him, and he mentally replayed her last statements. "You're what, the premier scholar in ancient Sumerian?"

Of course a hundred dollars is probably two or three months' rent here, he thought, and those signed firsts won't be worth fortunes for a while yet, here.

"No," she said, "that'd be Samuel Kramer at the University of Pennsylvania. I'm not the best translator, per se, but I'm the best translator for the purposes of my employers. For them it has to be someone who has done effective—*a*ffective—work in rhyme and meter, they want the translation to have the authority rhyme and meter have. And—"

"Rhyme and meter," echoed Blanzac. He was peering mistrustfully out at the skyline, but he forced himself to pay attention. "Uh—isn't that kind of old fashioned?" He preferred free verse poets like Sylvia Plath. "Even… now?"

Salvage and Demolition

"Oh hell, Vader, *beer* is old fashioned, *salt* is old fashioned. Why do you think magic spells in stories always rhyme? And kids' jump-rope rituals? And political slogans? The subconscious, the pre-rational part of your brain, thinks a statement must be important if it rhymes. And meter, that drum-beat— imagine how *un*inspiring the St. Crispin's Day speech in *Henry V* would have been if it wasn't in iambic pentameter!"

The cab had swept through the dimly-lit Columbus Street intersection and the engine was louder now as the driver downshifted for the climb up Russian Hill.

"And," she went on, "the parts I've been assigned apparently have to be translated by a woman. Most Sumerian script is in a dialect called *eme-gir,* but certain mystery-cult poems are written in another, called *eme-sal,* a special dialect that was ascribed to women. The poem has several sections in *eme-sal,* and my employers had me translate all of them, though that's a good deal more

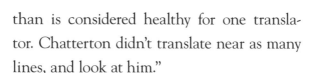

than is considered healthy for one translator. Chatterton didn't translate near as many lines, and look at him."

Blanzac nodded, leaning back now and just frowning out the window at the slanted-looking buildings they passed. "Tell me about this duplicate of me."

"Keep your fluffy little pants on, I'm getting there. Of course men can translate the *eme-sal* sections, but the Sumerian script has a lot of homonyms, words that are spelled the same but have different meanings. At those points the translator has to just intuit the intended meaning, and my employers believe the job requires a woman, a woman poet, to divine the intended flow."

"Chatterton, you said? Not the 18th century suicide?"

"Yes." She slid the partition aside as the cab turned south on Divisadero and said to the driver, "That's it on the left."

The night had got chillier, and when they had got out Blanzac shivered on the sidewalk

in his light corduroy jacket as Greenwald paid the driver.

Stepping up to the gate of the turreted old apartment building, she said, "I'm on the top floor, in what used to be Larry Ferlinghetti's flat; he and his wife are living over on Chestnut now."

"Ferlinghetti? The poet Ferlinghetti?"

"That's the one."

The thought of Lawrence Ferlinghetti still in his forties, without a white beard, made Blanzac think of his own parents— in 1957 they were newly married, and living in a rented house in Richmond across the bay.

"What's the date?" he asked Greenwald as she swung open the wrought-iron gate.

"April seventeenth."

And my mother, he thought, age twenty, is over there in Richmond right now, pregnant with her first, my older brother! I'm not even going to be conceived for another fourteen years!

"Let's get inside," he said, suddenly afraid that his twenty-one-year-old father might somehow drive down Divisadero and see him—a figure who shouldn't exist here, now—and be, to some initially small but incrementally escalating extent, nudged out of his predestined course.

III

AT THE TOP of two flights of narrow stairs, Greenwald's apartment was three rooms: a hexagonal living room with three tall windows overlooking the street, a bedroom, and a tiny kitchen. There might have been a bathroom, but Blanzac didn't immediately see a door for one. In the living room, two standing lamps with parchment shades threw a mellow glow over mismatched rugs, an old table and

couch and overstuffed chair, and high shelves haphazardly filled with books. Between the windows hung unframed abstract paintings. The room smelled of oranges and dusty central heating.

Greenwald waved Blanzac toward the chair and hurried into the kitchen, emerging a moment later with a half-full bottle of Gordon's gin and a glass.

"Damn it, I'm still too sober," she said as she sat down on the couch and twisted the cap off the bottle. She tipped it up for a couple of swallows right from the neck of it, then splashed several inches of gin into the glass. "They can sense my thoughts when I'm clear-headed—even what direction I'm in, from them. I've read *way* too much of that damn poem, and so have they. It's an inconvenient link." She clanked the bottle onto the table and gulped a mouthful from the glass and then scowled at Blanzac. "I don't know why *you're* drunk, they don't have hooks into *you*."

Blanzac wondered uneasily how unstable she might be. "Who?" he ventured. "And what sort of hooks do they have in you?"

"The poem, the translation! My employers, they work for—they're disciples of—this fake Swami Rajgah, the self-unrealization guru, who is due back in town tomorrow. He's dying of cancer, you see, so they're all in a hurry."

Blanzac shrugged. "Okay."

She gigled and drank some more gin. "Have you ever heard of Philipp Mainlander? German philosopher, killed himself in 1876? No? He had the idea of a god that did the same thing, killed itself, before time started, though I guess 'before' doesn't mean anything in that context. My employers think it's true, and lately I think so too. Alan Ginsberg can translate Latin, and they offered him the job of translating parts of a late Latin version of the poem, but he turned 'em down, said he wouldn't participate. He said the god was this primeval Mayan deity called Akan, who was apparently always portrayed cutting off his own head; but every culture, in their oldest mythologies, has been aware of it. In Egypt it was remembered as Aker, the god who had to be asked for permission to go to the underworld, and in the oldest European cults it was the Horned God."

She paused, so Blanzac nodded. "Old suicide god," he said. "I'm with you."

"One theory," she went on, "is that this god was sort of an anti-particle to the Judeo-Christian God. Opposite in every way, including in the wish to exist. Which it decided not to. Supposedly it left a— what you could call a hole in reality, shaped like itself, as it were, and—and if you cram a whole lot of people into an empty round room with a domed ceiling, pile 'em on top of each other till there's no more empty space left, you've got a mass of protoplasm in the shape of a cupcake."

Blanzac wondered where he could go, if Greenwald became downright crazy. Not to his eventual parents' house in Richmond, for sure. Maybe he could find some mission for the homeless, south of Market Street...

"...I suppose so," he said.

"But it's still a gap in the architecture." She gave him a haggard smile. "I'm not making sense, am I?"

Blanzac spread his hands. "Not so's anybody'd notice."

"Was you ever stung by a dead bee?"

At that Blanzac laughed, cautiously relieved, for it was a quote from the Bogart movie *To Have And Have Not*.

"They can still sting you," he said, trying to quote the Walter Brennan character accurately, "especially if they was mad when they died."

Greenwald sighed and sat back. "I guess this old dead god was mad. I'm afraid he's stung me." She stared across the table at him. "And then *you* showed up a few hours ago. From the future, allergedly. Allegedly. Why are *you* here?"

"I have no idea." He didn't want to get into speculations that would surely involve the fact that she was to die in 1969. "I was sitting at my desk in 2012, and then I was sitting on nothing in that restroom hallway. But you say you talked to me this afternoon, right? I guess I didn't have any explanation then either?" She shook her head, and he went on, "I think you'd better tell me about the *me* you met today."

"Okay." Greenwald reached across and touched his hand with one unsteady finger, as if to make sure he was physically present. "This afternoon my boss and a couple of the Swami's fellows tried to grab me and throw me into a car, on North Point Street by the Ghirardelli chocolate factory, but there were people around—a drunk on the other side of the street had just yelled something at me, and there was a woman walking a dog who started yelling, I mean the woman, not the dog, well, the dog was barking too, and then you were there right next to me, and you pulled me away from my, my would-be kidnappers. You threw a cup of coffee in one of them's face, and the lady and the dog were still yelling and barking, and Devriess, the guy you threw coffee at, cussed and got back in the car and took off." Her finger was still touching his hand. "And then you and I had some Irish coffee, and then we came back here, and—and—well, it *is* 1957, and you *had* just saved me from maybe torture, and you were...a lot more charming than you are tonight."

He opened his mouth, uncertain of what he should say here, but she stood up and crossed to the nearest window and pulled the long curtain across the view of the night sky.

"And you said," she went on briskly, returning to the couch and sitting farther away from him, "that it was the second time you had met me; you told me you first met me at the Tin Angel *tonight*—though, when you said it, tonight was still a couple of hours in the future. And you knew everything I'm telling you now, and you warned me that when

I met you tonight you wouldn't know any of it. You came with me to the bar tonight, but when it was time for *you* to appear, in the rest room hallway, you left by the front door. I didn't believe your story until you damn well *did* appear from the hallway, and you really *didn't* know any of this stuff." She leaned forward, and Blanzac guessed she had looked at the clock on the stove when she added, "You said you disappeared from here tonight at around ten. We've got an hour or so yet."

He stared at her, dizzy to realize that, at least at this moment, he believed her. If it was possible for him to fall into the past at all, it wasn't implausible that he would touch down in a couple of places like a skipped stone, and not in the local chronological order. At last he said, "And I told you my name is Richard Vader."

"Yes. Isn't it?"

If I did prevent a kidnapping this afternoon, he thought—if that event really does lie in my personal retrograde future, though in this world's immediate past—it may have called attention to me, among some dangerous-sounding people.

And they might still succeed in grabbing her, and she might tell them my name. I certainly don't want anyone, even just her, interfering with any Bay Area people named Blanzac.

"Yes," he said.

"Hmm. Well, Vader will do, I suppose. You didn't tell me much about what's going to happen. You're supposedly from...fifty-five years in the future! I gather the United States still exists."

"Uh, yes. And the Soviet Union has collapsed." What else? The Kennedy assassinations? 9-11? A list of presidents?

"Do you know a Betty Barlow?" he asked finally.

Greenwald blinked. "She's a friend of mine, works at the Discovery bookstore on Columbus. We're always planning to go to Mexico together someday. Why?"

"I just figured you'd know her. Along with Ferlinghetti and Ginsberg and all." He glanced at the two uncurtained windows. "Won't these swami boys come looking for you here?"

"No. They, my employers, have an old address of mine, and I get mail at a post office box, and this place is rented under somebody else's name."

A big long-haired calico cat walked out of the bedroom, stretched one hind leg straight out behind it for a moment and then yowled reproachfully. Greenwald sighed and stood up.

"Keep your fluffy little pants on," she told the cat as she walked back into the kitchen. "She doesn't live here, but I've got to feed her," she called over her shoulder. "I'll be back in a moment."

As the cat trotted after her toward the kitchen, it occurred to Blanzac that it did seem to have fluffy pants on. He heard the pop and *grind, grind, grind* of a manual can opener being worked, and he leaned back in his chair and looked at the bookcase.

He could see a copy of Ginsberg's *Howl*, and he was sure that it was a first edition, signed, and that he knew what the inscription was.

And he recognized a stack of five paperbacks as having the red-and-blue striped spines of Ace Double novels; he stood up and crossed the old carpet to the bookshelves and picked up one of the copies—noting that all five were identical—and he wasn't surprised to see that it was *Seconds of Arc* on one side and *What Vast Image* on the other.

"I already gave you a copy of that, this afternoon," Greenwald remarked, wiping her hands on a towel as she walked back to the couch, accompanied by a whiff of tuna. She looked at the table and then at the floor. "It's around here someplace. I wrote both the novels, and Alan Ginsberg got Ace Books to publish the pair after he made a deal with them for a William Burroughs book. I swore Alan to secrecy, and I thought the pseudonym would hide me, but I guess my damned *employers* found my name in the copyright office. They bought up just about the entire run, and burned them."

Blanzac was peering at the byline on one of the lurid covers. "Unless I'm mistaken—" he said slowly, "and no, I'm not mistaken!—they probably didn't have to go to the copyright office. 'Daniel Gropeshaw' is an anagram of Sophia Greenwald."

She looked crestfallen. "My God, is it that obvious? Auctorial vanity—it *is* my work, and I suppose I just couldn't resist putting at least a disguised version of my name on it."

Blanzac shook his head impatiently. "So who *are* these, these *employers* of yours?—who want to *kidnap* you? And why did they burn all the copies of this? And—some kind of *swami*?"

She picked up a pack of Camels from the table and held it toward him; he took one, though they were unfiltered, and he leaned forward to the match she held out after she had lit one of her own.

"It's the damned *poem*," she said, exhaling smoke. "They've been trying to get it effectively translated for…God, at least three hundred years. They had Christopher Smart and Thomas Chatterton trying to unravel the Latin version in the 18th century, but nobody knew then that it's like exposure to radiation, you can't have one translator do too much of the thing, or he gets sick, his perceptions get screwy, he pretty much goes nuts." She gave Blanzac a bright-eyed smile. "*I've* done more lines than I should, and that's from the original Sumerian, all the sections of it that are in the *eme-sal* dialect! Chatterton got a lot of the Latin version translated, but he apparently had a moment of sanity, and destroyed his manuscript and then killed himself."

Blanzac managed to catch his cigarette when it fell out of his mouth. "What the hell *is* it?"

"It was ogrig—'scuse me—*ori*ginally a cuneiform text on ten big limestone tablets in a place called Al Hillah in Iraq, used to be Babylon. Crusaders from Levantine Edessa destroyed the tablets in 1098, but a French clerk had copied out the inscriptions, and there was already a fairly messy Greek translation, and Irenaeus had quoted a few lines in one of his treatises against heresies in the second century. And a differently-messy Latin translation showed up in the 15th century, apparently rendered from the Greek but with some fixes that imply acquaintance with the original. *And—*"

She paused to take a long drag on the cigarette and a hasty gulp of the gin. "And," she went on hoarsely through the smoke, "What the poem is, is the definition, the *apologia pro deletu meo,* of this god that killed itself before the beginning of time. The images— no, the reader's *responses* to the images, to the kamikaze *theses* and *antitheses* of the poem's dialectic—lead the reader to the negating *synthesis* which this god consisted of. It's a *reductio ad nihilum.* And if enough people read the thing all at about the same time, like in a newspaper, then—"

"Ah," said Blanzac, "they fill in the empty room?"

Greenwald frowned at him. "What room? Are you too drunk to follow what I'm—"

"We're both on the same drunk wavelength," he assured her. "I mean what you said before, cram a whole lot of people into an empty round room—"

"Oh, right. Sorry. Yes, all together they take on the shape of the empty space. The god, call it Akan, is still dead, still absent, but their clustered living minds take on what you could call its shape, its features, like water filling a particular circuitous dry riverbed. A sort of Moebius riverbed."

"It's like the SETI project," said Blanzac, half to himself. "They need a supercomputer that's too big for anybody to ever actually make, so they get a million volunteers to remotely connect their little individual computers together." He squinted at her as if against a headwind. "What happens to the people?—who read the poem in the paper?"

"Well, it's never happened before. Maybe they'd just have a blackout as the god's lifeless shape passed across them, and be fine again next day. Maybe they'd all go crazier than Smart and Chatterton. Maybe they'd all spontaneously die, from being pieces of the mosaic that filled in the dead god's spiritual outline."

Blanzac shook his head dubiously. "Why would your swami want this to happen?"

"He's not a covert Communist, if that's what you're thinking. He, and his aides, his disciples, want to read the poem themselves, shortly after a whole lot of other people have read it—they hope to ride the wave of helplessly conforming minds right into...the state Akan is in, though you can't really use the verb 'is' about Akan. Nonexistence." She opened her mouth as if searching for another word, then just repeated, "Nonexistence."

"Well, what—why don't they just kill themselves? Like their god did? Why the—"

"That wouldn't get them nonexistence! It did for this god—it's the essence of Akan not to exist, it's the definition of it—but for humans to achieve that, they have to fall sideways through that god-shaped hole, right out of reality! If they just *die*, suicide or not—and over the centuries most of them *have* died without the escape hatch of the poem—they go on to whatever the afterlife is. And Swami Rajgah is supposed to be in the last stages of cancer, so he needs the poem to be armed and fired right away."

"They're scared of—what, Hell?"

Blanzac jumped then, and lost his cigarette again, for the front door lock snapped and the door swung open and a dark-haired young man in a gray suit and tie stepped into the room. He was holding a revolver pointed at the carpet.

"Miss Greenwald," he said, and his voice seemed to have a trace of some European accent, "you are insufficiently drunk." Then he noticed Blanzac and hastily raised the revolver. "Remain sitting, my friend—you've no coffee to throw tonight, eh?"

Greenwald eyed the intruder warily. "You're too late, Devriess," she said. "Did you think I wouldn't burn it, after your tricks this afternoon? Get another poet and start over."

Devriess leaned toward her and sniffed, then smiled. "Your anxiety is too...immediate. You fear that I will find it, not that I will administer some penalty."

Another man, heavier and older and wearing a tan overcoat, had stepped in beside Devriess. "It's her best work," he said. "She won't have burned it." He crossed to the bookshelves, keeping a wary eye on Blanzac, and picked up one of the Ace Double paperbacks.

"Look," he said, "she even squirreled away a pile of these." He glanced down at the book—"The inoculation," he sneered, "hah!"—and tossed it back onto the others. He put his arm out straight and began slowly to turn around. "Tell me when I'm getting warm," he said.

Devriess sniffed the air over Greenwald's head again, and after a few moments said, "Stop."

His partner's hand was pointing at a hi-fi console below one of the windows, and the man crossed to it and knelt to pull open one of the doors of the cabinet below the turntable. He fumbled inside and then slid out a wooden box like a cigar humidor, and when he swung back the lid Blanzac glimpsed a stack of papers inside, and lines of handwriting on the top sheet.

"That's it," said Devriess. "She is very not happy."

His partner rolled the manuscript into a thick cylinder and straighted up, holding it in one hand.

"Damn you," whispered Greenwald. "You might go to Heaven, Valhalla, Paradise, the Elysian Fields…!"

"And see, there," agreed Devriess with a brightly false smile, "and act, and comprehend, and think! 'When but to think is to

be full of sorrow and leaden-eyed despairs'—
Non, merci." To his companion he said, "carry
the inoculation book away too."

The older man nodded and with his free
hand shoved the five paperbacks into various
pockets of his overcoat.

Devriess stepped back toward the open
door. "You can even now come along," he said
to Greenwald. "We do not hold this against
you. We do not hold anything."

"Non, merci," she said through clenched
teeth.

"Certain? How is your vision, depth perception, your memory? No irrational rages,
fears, dreams of falling? The candle is not
burning so unevenly as to merit blowing out?
'To cease upon the midnight with no pain'?
No?" He shrugged, beckoned to his companion who was carrying the manuscript, and
both of them stepped out into the hall, pulling the door closed.

Greenwald snatched up the gin bottle and
took several gulps as the two men's footsteps

receded down the stairs, and Blanzac winced at the juniper reek of it. He opened his mouth, but she made a sharp chopping motion to silence him.

At last they heard the building's front gate slam and footsteps knocking on the sidewalk, and she exhaled and glared at Blanzac.

"*You son of a bitch,*" she whispered, "*why didn't you tell me about that?* You told me I'd meet you tonight, and that we'd come back here, and that you'd disappear—why didn't you tell me that they'd come and *take the manuscript?* I could have—*" She shook her head and spat.

"*I* don't know!" protested Blanzac. "I don't know that I *do* come back here earlier today! But if I do, I'll tell you this time, I promise—"

She blinked. "You'll…tell me? This afternoon? But no, if you tell me—" And then abruptly she was laughing, and she got up from the couch and leaned over him to give him a messy gin-flavored kiss on the mouth. "I'm sorry!" she said, smiling down at him.

"They'd have known, if—you see? They'd have *known,* if I'd hidden it somewhere else! I *believed* they were taking the Akan translation, and Devriess could *sense* that I believed that. Did it look like my handwriting, in that box they took?"

Blanzac had not got a close look at the top page in the box. "I don't know," he said, "I'm not—"

"Never mind, you wouldn't know, would you—but it looked like it to Devriess, so it probably was. What would I—" She snapped her fingers. "I bet I know what it was! It was probably my old translation of Hesiod's *Theogony.* Wait a moment."

She straightened up and swayed into the bedroom, and a few moments later came out again waving a lidless cardboard box in one hand.

"It's empty all right," she said, frowning and nodding. "My Hesiod translation was in this. I took a shower this afternoon, and you were alone for ten minutes—you will be, that is, from your point of view—and you must have put the Hesiod manuscript into that box." She waved at the now empty wooden box beside the hi-fi cabinet.

She stared at him fiercely. "You've got to do that, you understand? This is probably why you were sent here from the future! Come in here."

He followed her into the bedroom and she pointed to an empty space between two books with German titles on a crowded bookshelf over her narrow bed. "That's where this box was," she said with careful articulation. She held the cardboard box up to the gap to make it clear. "Right? When I'm in the shower a couple of hours ago, you've got to come in here, take the papers out of this box, and put them into that wooden box they emptied. Right? Okay?"

Blanzac was dizzy and his mouth tasted of second-hand gin, and wanted to go sit down again. "Okay," he said. "And what do you want me to do with the, the Akan translation?—after I take it out of the wooden box in the stereo?"

"Stereo! Hide it. Uh, hide it under my pillow, all right? This pillow right here." She pointed at the bed.

Blanzac shrugged. "Okay."

Greenwald lifted the pillow. There were no papers under it.

"What the hell!" she said. "I just told you to put it there!"

Blanzac spread his hands. "Maybe you change your mind about where to hide it. That's not a very good place, really."

"It's good enough, we know they didn't search the apartment. Dammit—okay, hide it under the sink in the bathroom, will you do *that?*"

"Sure."

They shuffled through a doorway into a closet-sized bathroom, and when Greenwald hiked up her black dress and sat down on the green-and-white tiled floor and opened the low cabinet, Blanzac had to step into the still-damp shower. His shoulder clinked a couple of shampoo bottles together on a tile shelf, and he realized they were glass.

"It's not in here, either," said Greenwald, her voice muffled, "though you'd have had plenty of room!" She sat back and scowled up at him. "What the *hell* did you *do* with it?"

"Maybe in a minute you're going to tell me to burn it, and so this afternoon I threw it down the incinerator shaft! Have you got those in this building?"

"Yes, but my God, don't do that!" She got to her feet and smoothed out the black dress. "It's the only copy, and—and all my notes on the Sumerian grammar are in there too, and carbons of Christopher Smart's version—"

Blanzac stepped out of the shower. "You want it *preserved*?"

"No, I just don't want it destroyed! Jesus! I'm not sure the originals of the Smart lines still exist anywhere. *Don't* do that, even if I tell you to in the next—" She glanced at the kitchen clock, "in the next hour!" She

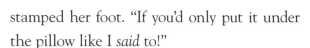
stamped her foot. "If you'd only put it under the pillow like I *said* to!"

"I still could," he said; then he grimaced and added, "no, sorry, right, it'd be there now."

She didn't seem to have heard him. "Maybe," she said slowly, "it's good *not* to have it in the apartment. Hesiod's not a bad decoy, but one of those guys might be familiar with the Latin version of my text, and see that what they took isn't part of that. Swami Rajgah will know, for sure, when they show it to him." She was snapping her fingers rapidly. "We've got to get out of here right now, out of town, I can't come back here. I'll take the Fleming book. Can you drive a car?"

"Sure." He took a deep breath and let it out. He was suddenly feeling dizzy. "Maybe after some black coffee."

"I've got my sister's Volkswagen in the garage downstairs, but I can't drive anymore, 'specially at night. No depth perception, misinterpretation of images. Wages of sin. Wages of Sumerian. We'll think of a place outside the building for you to hide it." She watched as he stepped carefully to the couch and sat down. "Come on, Murgatroyd, they might be back here any second!"

"Right, right." He sighed and pressed down on the arm of the couch, but it seemed to yield under his palm like brittle foam, and for a moment he caught the familiar whiff of coffee and book paper from his office in 2012.

He held still, then cautiously inhaled—and there were only the faint citrus and burnt dust smells of Greenwald's apartment. The upholstered arm of the couch was solid again, but he didn't put any weight on it.

"I think I'm…going," he said. His voice was a careful monotone. "Disappearing."

"What, right now? It's earlier than you said! But *where's the manuscript?*"

He heard a telephone ringing—the resonance sounded oddly constricted in the big volume of Greenwald's living room, and its tone was recognizably that of the one on his own desk.

"You don't hear a phone ringing," he said quietly, not daring to move.

"No." She knelt beside him and reached out as if to take his hand, then hesitated, apparently fearful that touching him might hasten his disappearance. Tears glittered on her eyelashes. "Look—just make sure they don't get it, okay?"

He nodded, shaking her living room out of focus for a moment. "I'll see you earlier today."

"But *I* won't see *you* again—maybe ever!" She grabbed for his hand, and her hand went through his as if through a shadow, and just thumped the upholstery; and as the couch gave way beneath him he caught four last fading syllables which might have been, "Read what I wrote!"

He raised his arms and straightened his legs to keep from falling, and then the light shifted and he was hopping to keep his balance on the carpet in his office. His hands slapped against his desk and he turned around and leaned against it.

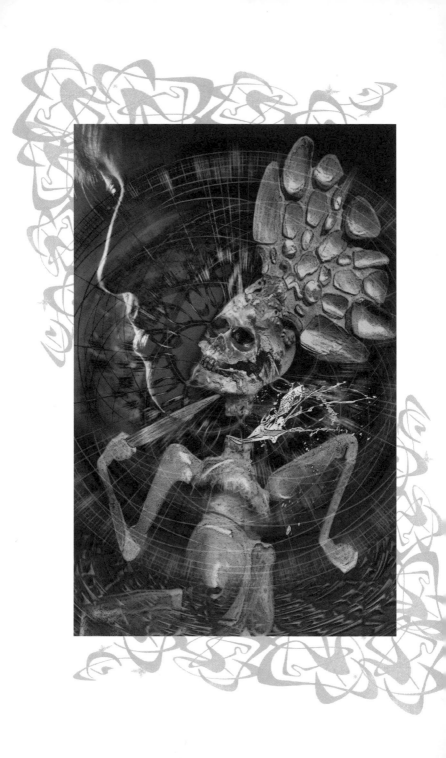

IV

HE WAS BREATHING hard and squinting around at the familiar shelves and file cabinets, which were still lit by early evening sunlight slanting in through the window. A round section was missing from the carpet, and some pieces of the vanished chair lay in a dished concavity in the exposed floorboards. The nearest bookshelf showed a round patch of pale shaved wood across the shelf edges, and the sewn quires of a book deprived of its spine. That Hemingway is worthless now, he thought automatically, and that was a first-state dust jacket.

There were no fragments of Greenwald's couch on the floor. Apparently the bounce-back had returned only himself to the present, not any surrounding bits that belonged to the past. He was at least still wearing his clothes.

The telephone was still ringing, and he picked up the receiver. He tried to say Hello, but could only pant into the mouthpiece.

From up the hall came the bong of the doorbell, and from the phone Blanzac heard a man's voice: "Mr. Blanzac, this is Jesse Welch, we met half an hour ago at the Goldengrove Retirement Community. I noticed on your business card that you're on my way, and I thought I'd stop by to take a quick look at the Greenwald items."

"Just a minute," Blanzac said, "there's somebody at my front door."

Welch chuckled. "That's me. My route home takes me right past your exit, so I thought, Why not visit? Could I have just a few minutes of your time?"

With an unreasoning chill, Blanzac remembered Welch's question half an hour ago: *Did the consignment include any manuscripts that might be Greenwald's?*

"A minute of my time," echoed Blanzac as he hastily made a decision. "Certainly! I—I just got out of the shower, I'll be with you as soon as I…throw on some clothes."

He hung up the phone, picked up the manuscript and the Ace Double paperback and shoved them over the top of a row of Einstein biographies on a high shelf so that they fell down behind the books, out of sight. Then he hurried down the hall to the kitchen and opened the door to the carport on the east side of the house; the kitchen door creaked, so he left it open as he stepped around the front of his white Chevy Blazer and carefully levered open the driver's side door. He got in and released the parking brake, and then, without closing the door all the way, he started the SUV and immediately shifted it into reverse and accelerated backward down the driveway.

Out in the street, while the vehicle was still rocking violently, he pulled the shift lever into Drive and stomped on the gas pedal; laughing with mingled alarm and embarrassment, he looked in the rear-view mirror and glimpsed someone moving from his front door toward the curb.

He swung left onto Washington Street; the lanes were clear and the sun was behind him now. There was an onramp for the northbound 280 ahead, and if he could get onto that freeway without Welch seeing the move, he should be safely lost in the infinite every-which-way traffic of the San Franisco peninsula...if in fact his anxiety was justified and Welch was indeed trying to follow him.

A police car passed him going the other way, and Blanzac lifted his foot from the accelerator. He told himself to drive carefully—he had left his wallet, again, on his desk at home, and in any case he was still somewhat drunk, from bourbon he had drunk fifty-five years in the past.

The receptionist at Goldengrove called Betty Barlow's room phone to ask if she was free to see her earlier visitor again, and, though the reply filled several seconds, she finally hung up the phone and told Blanzac, "She'll see you. Don't tire her or excite her."

"No," Blanzac assured her, though as he strode down the familiar hall he reflected that he was unlikely to follow that instruction. While crossing the Bay Bridge during the half hour drive from Daly City, an odd idea about old Betty Barlow had become a strong suspicion.

She was still lying in the bed when he stepped through the wide doorway into her room, and she was glaring in his direction from under her thin white hair. An overhead fluorescent light had been switched on since his last visit, dimming the light from outside and making the hour seem later.

"You again," she snapped. She peered around through her thick glasses. "You've burned the manuscript and the science fiction book? I want to see ashes."

"Keep your fluffy little pants on, Murgatroyd," he said. "I haven't been paid yet." He sat down in the chair beside the bed. "Remember that cigarette of mine that you put in your mouth this afternoon, and then gave back to me?"

"What? I *did* give it back to you. Did you come here again to get back one cigarette? You're drunk, I can smell it. Edith is a fool to have—"

"Yes yes, you gave it back to me. And I'm pretty sure I put that same cigarette in *my* mouth, when I got home," he said. "And it wasn't Betty Barlow I found waiting for me when the merry-go-round stopped. I'm—"

"Fluffy little pants," she interrupted, frowning past him. "That—that was about a cat."

"In your apartment on Divisadero," he agreed, "that Ferlinghetti used to live in." He took a deep breath and resolutely went on, "I imagine the authorities in a little Mexican town like Otatoclan don't really question the alleged identity of an American tourist who dies there, when they issue a death certificate. Especially back in 1969, when you didn't even need passports to be there."

The old woman's wrinkled face held no expression. After several seconds, she said, "That was a long time ago."

"Yes."

"I doubt anything could be established at this late date. Neither of us was ever fingerprinted."

"I imagine you're right."

"So why are you here?" Before Blanzac could frame an answer, she went on, "Isn't this the real manuscript, after all? Hah! Have you still just got, who was it, Hesiod? There's nothing I can do about it now. I swear to you I don't remember any of the Sumerian grammar or vocabulary anymore."

Blanzac shivered and stared at the withered old face on the pillow. Until this moment he had not truly believed that this really was Sophia Greenwald herself, the dark-haired young woman who had kissed him less than an hour ago, fifty-five years ago.

Blanzac said, gently, "I'm not one of the Swami's crowd, Sophie."

This time the silence lasted nearly a full minute, and if he hadn't seen her eyes blinking behind the thick lenses he might have thought she had gone to sleep.

"You have a young voice," she said finally. "But I might have heard it before today. *Blanzac* means nothing to me—who are you?"

Blanzac sighed and gripped his knees. "Back then I told you that my name was Richard Vader."

"Richard—?" She gasped and, in an oddly childlike gesture, she pulled the sheet up over her face.

"I wasn't going to see you," came her frail, scratchy voice through it, "if you somehow found me! And you *especially*, you were supposed to believe it was me that died in Otatoclan—Betty had no family, so it was easy to become her, after the cholera did her in, and then just stay in Mexico. *Rare books*—" She dropped the sheet and glared at him. "You said salvage and demolition!"

"I haven't said it yet," he told her. "I just fell out of your Divisadero living room half an hour ago. Devriess was just there, and took—probably took—your Hesiod translation." He spread his hands. "That was the evening. I'm apparently still due to go back, for the afternoon."

"Devriess!" she said with a visible shudder. "That's right, you arrived out of sequence, didn't you. What, that cigarette? This happened in the hour since you were last here?

And—and right now you've still got that afternoon ahead of you?" She rolled her eyes toward the ceiling. "Oh my." She shook her head sharply and looked at him. "Did you really just...find the manuscript in a box of papers? Lately?"

"This afternoon," he said. "This long afternoon."

"All this time, and *they* might have found it as easily as you! Where did you put it, on that day?"

"I don't know, I haven't done it yet."

"Where is it now?"

"Hidden in my office, at home. There's a guy who seems to want it—Welch? He even came to my house, half an hour ago. I ditched him and drove here. He said he was from the University of California."

"That you may be sure he was not. They still want it—Swami Rajgah died in '57, right on schedule, without finding his door into nothing, but his people still hope to find it, to save themselves...from existence." She tried to sit up in the bed, then fell back, panting. "You need to destroy it, Richard. Go straight home and burn it, please! I translated too much of it back then, and I think now it's… I'm very afraid that it's extending itself! In my dreams! Like crystals forming in salt water as it evaporates, as my mind is evaporating in this damn place. I'm afraid—I'm truly afraid that if they do it now, I'll be swept out through the hole with them! 'I have been half in love with easeful death,' but I want to, I *do* want to, take my memories with me, even if that means taking them to Hell."

"An hour ago you insisted that I *not* destroy it."

"Nonsense, the first thing I said to you here was—"

"Sorry, I mean in 1957. It was the almost the last thing you said to me before I fell back to now."

"Well, I was closer to it then. It was my work—hard work, good work. But it was evil work too. I had a gift, but I used it in the

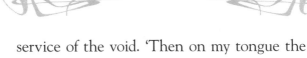

service of the void. 'Then on my tongue the taste is sour of all I ever wrote.'"

Blanzac stirred in his chair. "Your earlier work wasn't corrupted. Why keep it out of print?"

"Penance. Expiation."

"Don't you think the penance has gone on long enough? You said that your poetry was worthless. *Your* poetry, not the translation. Did you mean it?"

"Yes. I don't know. Who cares, now?"

"I think...you do. Do you believe it was worthless?"

"Why *ask?*"

"I think the answer is important. To you."

For several seconds she was silent; then she sighed heavily and pulled a Kleenex from a box on the table and took off her glasses to blot her eyes.

"No," she whispered. "It was as good as I could make it, and I was no slouch."

Blanzac opened his mouth to speak, but she went on quickly, "And the two science fiction novels—those were expiation too. They, published upside down to each other, they're made of images I believed would stay in a reader's head and deflect the disassembly-logic of the Sumerian poem, disarm its images by...*pre-emptively* hanging distracting contrary associations on them. The two novels are really the same plot, one set in the Amazon jungle and the other set in outer space, so I could use contrasting archetypes to fragment the Akan logic from all sides." She fitted her glasses back on. "And you still have the afternoon ahead of you, God help us! I wonder if this time you can do things differently than you did, and destroy it then."

Blanzac frowned and shook his head. "We wouldn't be talking about it now, if I had done it then. It's all happened already—I just haven't walked through my second-act part yet. First-act, I mean."

She waved a hand. "Of course," she said bleakly. "Free will versus determinism. That was the core contradiction behind the

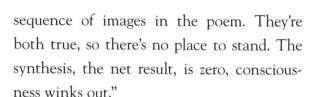

sequence of images in the poem. They're both true, so there's no place to stand. The synthesis, the net result, is zero, consciousness winks out."

"Really." Blanzac flexed his fingers. "You, uh, just explained it to me, and I'm still conscious."

"Well so am I, Murgatroyd," she said. It was the first time Blanzac had seen the old woman smile, and he winced as he recognized—for a moment, among the sagging wrinkles—the woman he had spent an hour with in 1957. "You need to read at least a good extent of the poem, visualize and vicariously experience each sequential juxtaposition of images, internalize them—the poem starts mild, and then escalates. Whoever put that thing together could have made Jung swallow his own head."

"Who *did* put it together?"

She sniffed. "You do smell like bourbon. You didn't *bring* any liquor, did you? Huh! Negligent. 'O for a draught of vintage!' Who put it together? It must have been a group, each man writing one section in the sequence. Astrologers maybe? And it must have been a relay team that cut the cuneiform into the Al Hillah limestone—or else somebody who couldn't read, and just copied the symbols."

Blanzac looked at her wrinkled, spotted hand on the bedsheet, and he remembered her touching his hand half a century ago.

"I should go," he said, standing up. "I'll burn the Akan text as soon as I get home."

She reached out a withered arm and turned the phone around to face him. "There's my number. Call me, please, as soon as it's surely gone."

He leaned forward and read the number taped onto the phone, and repeated it to himself.

"I've got it," he said, "and yes, I'll call you the minute it's done. But I'm going to get hold of your two poetry collections, and I hope you'll begin trying to find a publisher for them."

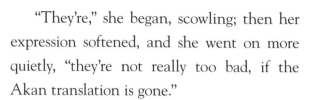

"They're," she began, scowling; then her expression softened, and she went on more quietly, "they're not really too bad, if the Akan translation is gone."

"We'll find a publisher," he told her, "or publish them ourselves. Get 'em on Amazon." He nodded and then left the room.

The sky was dark and the streetlights were on when he got home, and he paused in the kitchen to put a cup of water in the microwave oven. He noticed that he had left the kitchen door ajar, and he pulled it closed and locked it. Then the microwave binged, and he fetched down a jar of instant coffee and stirred a spoonful into the steaming water.

When, he wondered, do I go back to enact the 1957 afternoon? It was that cigarette that triggered the last jump, presumably because it had some of her saliva on it, constituted contact with her. Would I have jumped back if I had touched her during this last visit to Goldengrove?

It could be that I'll *stay* back there, this time, and simply disappear from 2012! I could go to Mexico with her—though tonight she talked as if I hadn't done that. Still, I should bring some things, have some useful items in my pockets—a gun, gold, a list of Kentucky Derby winners!

He picked up the coffee cup, blowing across the top of it, and hurried down the hall to his office.

He had taken two steps across the now-holed carpet and turned toward his desk, when he froze. In the dimness he could see two men standing by the bookshelves below the window.

"Mr. Blanzac," said one of them, "do please turn on the light."

Blanzac reached out to the side with his left hand and found the wall switch, and

when the overhead light came on he recognized Welch. The other man was very old—bald and stooped in a baggy lime-green leisure suit, blinking through bifocals and leaning heavily on an aluminum walker.

Welch, Blanzac noticed belatedly, was holding a revolver pointed at the floor.

The very old man began wheezing and trembling in frail excitement. "This is the fellow!" he croaked.

"What," said Welch, not taking his eyes off Blanzac, "you've seen him before?"

"He was with her, in San Francisco! He stopped us from capturing her—" The effort of speaking was making him drool. "He was with her when we—took what we *thought* was her translation!"

"That was in the '50s," said Welch irritably. "This isn't the same guy."

The old man's mouth was opening and shutting. "It was! It is! He's still young—"

"For God's sake, Devriess! Shut up." Welch raised the gun and pointed it at Blanzac's face. "We want the manuscript that was in that box. I'm sure it's here, and if I have to kill you I'll eventually find it, but you can save me some time. Oh, and your life."

But Blanzac was staring at the old man clinging to the walker. Devriess! He tried to recognize in this shaking, wet-eyed ruin the handsome young man who had politely taken Greenwald's Hesiod translation from the apartment on Divisadero fifty-five years ago.

"I really will kill you," remarked Welch. "And I really will find the manuscrpt, afterward. I imagine it's right in this room."

"Yes," said Blanzac, exhaling. If I had any hope, he told himself, of saving Sophie's soul by resisting here, I might resist; but he *would* find the manuscript, in any case.

He slowly put the cup down on the desk, and raised his hands. "I've got to pull some books down from a high shelf."

Welch nodded. "Pull down a gun and you'll be dead before you can aim it."

Blanzac nodded too, then turned around and reached up for the Einstein biographies. He gripped half a dozen of them and pulled them out, then crouched to set them on the carpet; he straightened up and reached in behind where they had been, and when he turned around again he was holding the sheaf of manuscript.

He laid it on the desk and picked up his coffee and stepped back to take a cautious sip of it. "So now what?" he asked. "You get a lot of people to read it, so you can step out of reality?"

Welch had relaxed at the sight of the stack of papers, and he smiled. "I wasn't actually sure you had it! Yes, lots of people." He waved toward Devriess. "Their plan back in the '50s was to buy a few pages of a magazine and publish the thing that way, but we're ready to hack it into a thousand high-traffic online blogs. Millions of people will read it on the same morning!" Assuming a Peter Lorre accent, he said, "And then, *adio* Casablanca."

Blanzac laughed, for he had all at once dizzily decided to try to take the gun away from the man. "Your letters of transit," he said.

Welch smiled, nodding. "You played it for her," he said, in a Bogart imitation now, "you can play it for me." He shifted the gun to his left hand in order to reach for the stack of papers—and Blanzac lunged forward and with his free hand chopped down at Welch's wrist before the man could get his finger into the trigger-guard.

V

THE EDGE OF Blanzac's hand collided hard with the bones of Welch's wrist, knocking the man's arm sharply away—

And then the light was gone and the floor was tilted and Blanzac stumbled forward into a man who was somehow right in front of him. Blanzac had raised both hands to stop his fall, and he inadvertently splashed hot coffee into the stranger's face.

A cold wind that smelled of chocolate was blowing rain into Blanzac's eyes, and as

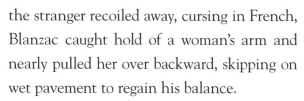

the stranger recoiled away, cursing in French, Blanzac caught hold of a woman's arm and nearly pulled her over backward, skipping on wet pavement to regain his balance.

Across the street—he was outdoors, he realized, on a street!—a woman was shouting and a dog was barking, and the woman Blanzac had grabbed was hastily stepping backward away from an old Buick idling at the curb, and she was pulling Blanzac back with her. His arm was tangled in the strap of her purse.

"Out of here!" came a muffled shout from inside the car—the passenger door was open—and the man Blanzac had splashed with coffee threw himself in across the seat.

The Buick roared and accelerated away, the tires leaving brief tracks on the wet asphalt. People on the other side of the street were staring and pointing and waving umbrellas, and one man had dropped a newspaper. Blanzac freed his elbow from the woman's purse-strap and peered at her in the dim street lamp glow.

She was Sophia Greenwald, again looking no more than thirty years old.

She blinked at him, then glanced across the street at the pedestrians on the opposite sidewalk. "Never mind," she said breathlessly, "let's get out of here."

"Where," he asked in a strangled voice as he matched her hurrying footsteps, "is here?" He waved his emptied coffee cup and then left it to fill with rainwater on a chest-level wall they were passing. "I mean, I bet it's San Francisco, but where?"

"North Point Street, by Ghirardelli. You know, the chocolate factory. Are you lost?" She looked over her shoulder, blinking against the rain. "Thanks for helping me, mister, but I should get out of sight."

What do I say? he thought. "Sophie, I can help you."

She paused, and after glancing narrowly up and down the street she looked closely at his face; she reached up and brushed the wet hair off his forehead with cold fingers, and

shook her head. "Who are you? I don't recognize you. Come on," she added, pulling him along and steering him around the lefthand corner onto the Hyde Street sidewalk. He could see the red neon Buena Vista sign shining against the gray overcast sky ahead of them. Beyond it through the veils of rain he could just see a cable car slowly rotating on the Hyde Street turnaround, with a man in a yellow raincoat pushing it.

Icy water was running down inside Blanzac's collar. "I believe we have some Irish coffee now," he said through clenched teeth.

She was still scanning the street, but she gave him a nervous smile. "I believe you're right."

They hurried down the slanted sidewalk to the Beach Street corner and Blanzac held open the door of the Buena Vista Café as she hurried inside.

He glanced at his hand on the door, and his jaw clenched in shock to see what appeared to be rain-diluted blood all over his right hand; with his other hand he slapped at his wrist and forearm, but felt no pain. He let the door close and hurried back across the sidewalk to a gushing rain-gutter and rinsed his hand, wiggling his fingers in the icy water. He flapped his arm, but no more red fluid appeared, and as far back as he could push the cuff of his jacket and shirt he could see no wound. Apparently it had not been blood, or not his, at any rate—perhaps young Devriess had been bleeding when Blanzac stumbled into him a few moments ago...though the man would seem uninjured when he would appear later this evening.

Blanzac heaved a deep sigh of relief and ran back to the Buena Vista door and pulled it open again.

The lights in the long yellow hall made the dark day outside the tall windows seem like night. Only a few people were sitting at the tables, but Greenwald had made straight for the tall wooden bar along the left-hand wall and was perched on a stool with her purse at her elbow, staring back at him. Getting his

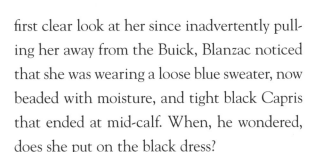

first clear look at her since inadvertently pulling her away from the Buick, Blanzac noticed that she was wearing a loose blue sweater, now beaded with moisture, and tight black Capris that ended at mid-calf. When, he wondered, does she put on the black dress?

He glanced at his watch—noting with a fresh surge of relief that there was still no blood to be seen—but then remembered that there would be no correspondence between his personal time and this local time.

"Do you," he began as he sat down on the stool next to her, then said to the bartender who leaned in, "Two Irish coffees, please. Wait, sorry, I don't have any money!" To Greenwald he said, awkwardly, "Order something if you like, I'll just...sit here and get warm."

"Don't be silly, you just saved me from God knows what, a kidnapping or something. Two Irish coffees, please," she repeated to the bartender. "And you started to say, 'Do you—'?"

"Oh, do you know what time it is?" He wished he had noted what time it was that he arrived—was to arrive—in the restroom hallway at the Tin Angel tonight.

She looked at her own wristwatch. "Five-thirty." As the bartender dropped sugar cubes into two glasses and poured coffee and Bushmill's whiskey into them, she squinted at Blanzac. "I still don't recognize you. How do you know me?"

"Ah, this will be hard to believe." Go ahead and be direct, he thought, you know it works out. "I'm from the future, from the year 2012. This right now," he said, tapping the bar, "is my second tumble back in time to this day, but they're out of order; on my *first* one I met you *tonight*—about three hours from how—at a bar called the Tin Angel."

She grinned delightedly and picked up her drink and took a sip of the fortified coffee through the cream layer on top, and there was a line of cream on her upper lip when she put it down and said, "Is it more like Pohl and Kornbluth in 2012, or Heinlein?"

Blanzac recognized the names of science fiction writers. "It's very like this, actually. Cars, gas stations, traffic signals, TV, movie theaters. The only difference you'd notice is that everybody in 2012 has a computer no bigger than a TV set."

She rested her elbow on the bar and cupped her chin in her hand. "Why do you all need computers? Are you forever calculating trajectories to other planets?"

He smiled and shook his head. "To write notes to each other, mainly. They're all hooked together via the phone lines."

She glanced at the dark windows and turned to face the bar. "So how do you really know me," she said in a level tone, "and who are you?"

"My name is—" He sighed. "—is Richard Vader. I was born in 1972, and I was an English major at San Francisco City College and got a BA in '94. I met you for the first time later this evening, and you told me about your translation work, the Sumerian poem."

She stood up, her face stony. "You leave right now, mister. When you're gone I'll call a cab."

Waving placatingly at the tensed bartender, Blanzac said with quiet urgency, "Sophie, I don't want it, I don't want to dive through the Akan hole! I very much want to help you keep it away from Devriess and Swami Gaga or whatever his name is."

"It's *Rajgah*." She eyed him skeptically but slowly resumed her seat. "Are you from the Vatican or something?" She shivered and hugged herself inside the wet sweater. "Well, I could *use* some help now, actually. But I gotta say it's a very outlandish sort of cover story you've chosen."

"I think you'd agree it's a pretty outlandish situation." He took a solid sip of the hot Irish coffee and sighed as the whiskey in it seemed to relax his chilled scalp. "Thanks for the drink. I'm afraid you buy me two more before the evening's out."

"A poorly equipped time traveler," she said. She opened her purse and took out a pack of Camels and slid an ashtray closer. "Didn't think to bring contemporary money, eh?"

"No wallet at all. I hadn't planned on coming." She held the pack of cigarettes toward him, and he took one. "Thanks," he said. "You can't smoke in public places anymore, in 2012." She struck a match and he leaned over her hand to get a light. "I was in my office at home both times, when with no warning I found myself," he said with an all-around wave of his cigarette, "here. 1957."

"Office? What do you do?"

"Uh—" He thought about the Sumerian manuscript. "Salvage and demolition, lately."

She had lit a cigarette of her own, and now her syllables were accompanied by little puffs of smoke. "So how is it that you know about the translation, and the Swami and Devriess?"

"You explain it all to me on my first visit—later tonight, starting when we're taking a cab from the Tin Angel back to your apartment." He smiled crookedly, remembering the conversation. "It's a fairly disjointed account, but eventually I get the story."

"You did stop Devriess just now from grabbing me and I don't know what, torturing me, maybe, to get the translation. But you didn't come here to help me, specifically."

"No, I fell into it somehow. But I landed squarely on your side." He paused for a moment. "I don't want," he went on, thinking of a frightened old woman in an assisted living home in 2012, "I *don't* want them to win."

"You said you landed on my side. I hope you're not kidding. There's nobody else on my side, and a big serious crowd against…us?"

"Us," he agreed.

She held out her right hand, and he shook it.

"Drink up, Captain Future," she said. "We should grab a taxi back to my place. You know where that is?"

"Divisadero, half a block south of Pacific."

She shivered again in her damp sweater. "I surely hope you're on my side—nobody's supposed to know that." She looked across at the bartender. "Could you call us a cab?"

"I think I'm going to have to leave town," she said as she closed the apartment door and clicked the wall switch that lit the two living room lamps, "at least for a while. I've completed my part of the translation—"

"The women's dialect," said Blanzac.

He had sat down on the couch, and she stepped into the kitchen. "Okay," she called, "now how do you know about that? Nobody knows about that except the Swami's crowd."

"And you. You tell me about it, in a few hours."

She came back into the living room carrying the bottle of Gordon's gin Blanzac had seen on his last visit here, visibly fuller now. "Live your cover," she said. "You don't want to say who you work for. I really hope you're a right guy, 'cause you're all I've got."

She picked up one of the stack of identical Ace Double science fiction novels—he noticed that there were six of them now—and waved it at him. "I wrote this," she said. "You should have a copy, it'll do you good." She shoved some books back to make room to set the bottle down, and then picked up a ball-point pen from the table and scribbled something in the middle pages of the book and tossed pen and book onto the table. Rain thrashed against the dark windows.

Bottle in hand again, she joined him on the couch and took another gulp of the gin. "You want some of this? I could get a glass. I have to stay fairly drunk at all times."

He nodded. "So they can't track you, because you've all read too much of the poem. No, I'm fine for now, thanks."

She put it down on the table beside an ashtray and pushed her wet hair back from her forehead with both hands. Blanzac felt the hairs on his arms stand up as he saw a *TV Guide* and a copy of the *San Francsico Chronicle* lying beside the ashtray. The cover of the *TV Guide* was a picture of Pat Boone.

"How long do you stay here today," Greenwald asked, "altogether?"

"I leave around ten, I think."

"Is there a Mrs. Vader, up there in the future?"

He smiled. "No."

"Never?" she asked, picking up the gin bottle again. "That's a long stretch of future." Bubbles gurgled up through the clear liquor as she drank.

"Never. I came close once, but she wanted me to be more ambitious. Big house with a pool, new cars…she eventually got a job with

Microsoft and found a guy like that." Seeing her raised eyebrows, he added, "Microsoft makes...things to do with computers."

"A square like that would be all wrong for you, Captain Future." Greenwald clanked the bottle down again. "What was her name?"

"Gillian."

"I hate her. I've got beer, if you'd rather."

"No, I—soon we'll be—" He paused, for her cold fingers were on his neck.

"You're all tense," she said, and began to knead the muscles of his shoulder under his wet collar. "And getting tenser! 'Tenser, said the tensor'! You don't like back rubs?"

He shifted around to face her, which pulled his shoulder free. Her hand fell onto the knee of his damp jeans. "Never got used to them," he admitted.

"God, we're both soaked." She stood up and looked away from him. "We should...get out of these damp clothes."

"Sophie," said Blazac unsteadily, "you've had a lot to drink—"

"I always do, these days."

"I'm apparently going to be disappear-ing—"

"Right, but then your three-hour-younger self will step in. So? Damn it, I'm not some—I'm thirty-one years old, and—and if we're—I need to know you. Right now you're a stranger."

"I'm afraid I'll never be much more than that," he said, but he got to his feet.

VI

WHEN SHE SLEEPILY got out of bed and said she'd take a shower before they left for the Tin Angel, Blanzac followed her into the bathroom and waited until she had turned on the water and stepped into the narrow shower stall—where he would be standing in a couple of hours while she looked for the manuscript under the sink—and then he hurried back to the bedroom. As he pulled on his clothes and shoved his feet into his shoes, he stole

glances at the furnishings of her room, and in that hurried moment the rocking chair and the framed pictures of silent-era movie stars and the couple of bowler hats on the wall all struck him as oddly endearing, and he wondered if he could be falling in love with Sophia Greenwald.

He found the box between the two German books on the shelf over the bed, quickly lifted out the sheets of the Hesiod translation, and slid the empty box back into its place on the shelf.

He was panting. Later tonight she would tell him that she stayed in the shower for ten minutes, and he hoped that was accurate.

There had to be another box, *the* box, ready to hand—he stepped into the living room and glanced around but didn't see one, then hurried into the kitchen. The window over the sink was open, and he nearly dropped the Hesiod papers when the calico cat startled him by leaping in and bounding to the floor, but after a few moments he found a box on the counter with three big 20-ounce jars of pickled garlic in it. He juggled them out one-handed and set them on the counter, then carried the box and the Hesiod translation into the living room and knelt to lay them on the carpet beside the hi-fi.

The wooden box was in the cabinet below the turntable, right where Devriess' companion would find it in an hour or so, and Blanzac pulled it out and opened it.

There was the remembered handwritten text—

As helplessly as shadows fall unfurled, he read, *To west instead of east as dusk comes on,/ As fated as the phases of the moon...*

—and he lifted the stack of papers out and dropped them into the cardboard box the jars of garlic had been in, then laid the Hesiod translation into the wooden box, closed it, and pushed it back in place and shut the cabinet doors.

Sweating, he stood up with the cardboard box in his hands.

And even though he knew he would be getting this box again in fifty-five years, the manuscript looked dangerously conspicuous all by itself in there.

He hurried to the table and tossed the Ace Double paperback in alongside the handwritten pages, and unfolded the outer sheet of the newspaper and threw that and the *TV Guide* in on top. For good measure he dumped the ashtray over it all, then folded the box's flaps closed and straightened up, holding it.

And he bared in teeth in agonized indecision. Where *was* he to put it? He couldn't hide it in the apartment, even though Devriess and his companion wouldn't search the apartment during their visit tonight; they might come back and do a thorough search when they discovered that what they had taken was the wrong manuscript, and it might not take them long to discover that.

Just throw it in a trash can on the street? But then he would not have got it in 2012, and would not visit the old woman who would claim to be Betty Barlow, and would therefore not be here now. If he removed himself from this chain of events, Greenwald would be alone when Devriess and that other man would come here tonight, and the Akan manuscript would be in the hi-fi cabinet.

Then he remembered her saying, *I've got my sister's Volkswagen in the garage downstairs, but I can't drive anymore,* and, *We've got to get out of here, out of town, I can't come back here.*

The Volkswagen will surely be returned to her sister somehow when Sophie disappears to Mexico, he thought. And the sister will apparently get the books, including the signed *Howl* and the Kerouac letters.

Greenwald had dropped her purse on the floor beside the couch, and he knelt by it and felt past her wallet and hairbrush and cigarettes to a set of keys at the bottom. One of the keys was a short brass Master, the only one that could fit a probable padlock on the garage door.

He pocketed the keys, opened the front door and carried the box down the stairs.

When Greenwald emerged from the steamy bathroom in a terrycloth robe, rubbing her hair with a towel, he had been standing by the bookshelves for thirty seconds, and he had stopped panting.

"Is that what you're going to wear to the Tin Angel?" she asked. "You don't seem to be drying out."

"I didn't bring a change of clothes," he said. "I'll be fine." He was holding a book in a gray dust-jacket with red hearts on it. "This is the British first edition of *Casino Royale*," he remarked. It hadn't been among the books he was to get in 2012.

She peered at it from under the towel. "Oh, Ian Fleming. Is it worth something?"

"It will be."

"Is he good? Maybe I'll take it with me."

"He'll—I think he'll write better books, but yes. Keep the dust-jacket in good condition." He put it back carefully.

She laughed. "Look at you, future boy, your fly's down and your shoes are untied. Fix up and I'll call for a taxi."

She disappeared into the bedroom as he hastily zipped his fly and sat down in the upsholstered chair to tie his shoes, and shortly she had emerged again wearing the remembered black dress and black leather pumps, brushing her hair.

"What do we do at the Tin Angel?" she asked.

"Well, I apparently disappear." He thought about the situation he had left in his office in 2012. "I don't know what happens to me after that. But then I'll appear out of the restroom hallway, but it'll be my first visit, the earlier me, who won't have met you yet and won't know any of the things we've talked about. I'll be pretty scared—I won't even believe it's

really 1957—I'll ask a guy at another table who's president, and even when he tells me Eisenhower I still won't believe it."

"You know, sweetie, you seem so sane most of the time." She shook her head as she stooped to pick up her purse. "We can wait downstairs in the entryway till we see the cab."

VII

WHEN THEY GOT out of the cab in front of the Tin Angel, Blanzac blinked around in the rain. In spite of everything, he was disoriented anew to see the Greenwich street sign at the corner.

She was holding the door for him, and he hurried forward. The air was warm inside and rich with the remembered smells of tobacco smoke and Beef Stroganoff, which

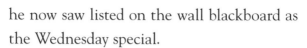
he now saw listed on the wall blackboard as the Wednesday special.

He led her down the long high-ceilinged room through the maze of tables to the one he remembered, and no one was sitting at it and the table was bare except for an empty ashtray.

"I'll get drinks," she said as he sat down.

"No," he said, catching her hand. "Sophie, there are drinks on the table when I come here for the first time—when I won't know you, and *this* me disappears. That can't happen until there's drinks."

She gave him a wry smile with her eyes half closed, but sat down. He still held her hand. "You won't remember this afternoon," she said.

"I won't have lived through this afternoon yet. *I'll* remember this afternoon as long as I live."

She squeezed his hand and then released it. "And you'll help, with this situation? The Swami, Devriess, the Akan translation?"

"I'll at least help, I can promise you that. You escape them, I promise."

"I hope so." She frowned, though still smiling. "Why—and if you won't say, I want to know why you won't say—*why* the story about coming from the future? How does that help?"

He shook his head, looking down at his hands. "It's the crazy truth. But I do want to tell you that I—"

She reached across the table and touched his lips. "Save it. I'll get drinks. What'll you have? I'm buying."

He opened his mouth, wanting to say that he loved her and that he wished it weren't impossible for them to stay together...

He sighed. "Bourbon on the rocks, as I recall."

She laughed softly and stood up.

He watched her step lithely away toward the bar, and he restrained a sudden impulse to run after her, hold onto her. She's going to be standing by the restroom hallway soon,

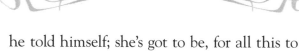

he told himself; she's got to be, for all this to work out.

Greenwald came back with two glasses and slid one in front of him as she took her seat.

"I suppose this earlier self of yours won't have any money either," she said.

"Thanks. No, both times I've left my wallet sitting on my desk, back home. Oh," he added, "and I once worked at a tobacco shop, and the boss's name was Ted."

She was squinting at him. "What?"

"It's true, and I apparently mention that to you. Covering all the bases here." He looked into her brown eyes. "You can't... imagine," he said with quiet intensity, "how much I wish I could stay here with you."

She nodded and looked away toward the back of the room. "1957 girls are easy. Were these drinks full, when you arrived here... now?"

"No. About half."

She picked up her glass and took several gulps. "Drink up," she said. "I think it's time I

met the other you. Hah! A line of iambic pentameter there for you to take away with you."

She pushed her chair back and got to
her feet.

He stood up too. "I'll go out the front," he
said. "You go stand by the hallway back there."

She nodded and turned away.

The floor began to wobble as he walked
to the street side door, and several of the people at the tables gave him irritated glances as
he lurched past them, and when he put out
his hand to take hold of the door handle, it
seemed to dissolve at his touch like a stack of
soap suds. He took a deep breath and stepped
forward, right through the closed door.

And then he was stumbling across the
carpet of his office, and Welch was spinning
away from him and rebounding off the desk,
and the revolver bounced off of the bottom
edge of a file cabinet.

Blanzac let his stumble become a crouch,
and he snatched up the gun and turned to
face the room.

Welch had slid off the desk and was now sitting on the floor, wheezing and clutching his left forearm; his left hand gleamed bright red with blood and his face was pale. Blanzac could see blood drops scattered across the desk top and falling rapidly now onto the carpet. He noticed that the hole in the carpet was more of an oval now, and bigger.

Old Devriess was just leaning on his walker by the window and gaping in confusion.

Blanzac shifted the gun in his hand. The bottom of the grip was oddly cut away on the left side, and it was awkward to hold.

Welch's mouth was opening and shutting, and finally he whispered, "I think you cut off my little finger!" His eyes darted around the diminished carpet. "Where is it? They can sew it back on." He squinted up at Blanzac. "What did you cut me with?"

Blanzac remembered the blood he had belatedly noticed on his hand outside the Buena Vista Café. "You're lucky," he panted, swallowing hard against nausea, "that I was knocking your hand *away,* when I touched you. Otherwise—you'd probably have lost the whole hand."

But why, he wondered, should touching *him* have propelled me back? What intimacy have I ever shared with *him*—especially in 1957?

Blanzac glanced at Devriess. "Who is he?" he asked, waving the gun at the bleeding figure sitting on the floor. "Where did you recruit him?"

A sigh. "Far from here, long ago."

Blanzac crossed cautiously to the desk and with his free hand shook out one sheet of the old *San Francisco Chronicle* and laid it out flat. "Tell him where his missing finger is."

Devriess rocked his bald head back and stared at the ceiling. "It is probably in the gutter on North Point Street. Or it was, fifty-five years ago." He lowered his head and gave Blanzac a frail smile. "The coffee cup you were holding a moment ago—it is there too, yes?"

"Overflowing with rainwater by now," Blanzac agreed. He lifted the stack of papers that were the Akan translation and laid them in the middle of the big square of newsprint.

"Find my goddamn *finger*," Welch sobbed, scuffing his heels on the carpet.

The revolver was shaking in Blanzac's fist. "It's in San Francisco!" he said, more shrilly than he'd meant to. "Weren't you listening? Fifty-five years ago!"

Looking at Welch's contorted face and sweaty gray hair, Blanzac thought: Fifty-five years ago. And touching him propelled me back there.

He glanced across at Devriess and then back at Welch.

"Welch," said Blanzac slowly, forcing his voice to be level, "listen to me. I'll let you two leave, so you can get to a hospital. But first, throw me your wallet."

"Screw you. Find my finger!" The man's face was as pale as old bedsheets, and gleaming with sweat.

"Throw me your wallet or bleed to death right there." After a few seconds he added, "I've got all night."

Whining, the older man loosened his grip on his wrist to reach around behind himself, and then he threw a wallet onto the carpet and clutched his wrist again. "Take it," he said hoarsely. "I'll cancel all the credit cards."

Blanzac crouched, picked up the wallet, and flipped it open as he straightened up. He glanced again at Devriess, who rolled his eyes and nodded.

Jesse Lewis Welch had been born on January 20, 1958. May, June, July—yes, almost exactly nine months later.

"We adopted, yes, *recruited* him," said Devriess quietly, "as a possible lever." He shrugged. "But we could not find her, and when we learned where she was, nine years later, it was because she had died."

Blanzac's chest felt hollow as he turned to stare at the gray-haired, bloody, dishevelled figure of Welch sitting on the blood-spattered carpet. Blanzac ached to say something important, but after standing with his mouth open for ten seconds, "You deserved better," was all he could think of. He added, "From me, from everybody."

Then he folded the newspaper around the manuscript and tucked the bundle under his arm; the posture meant he couldn't swing the gun from one man to the other as easily, but neither looked aggressive right now.

Finally Blanzac stretched out his free arm, reached into the box and lifted out one of the old Camel cigarette butts.

"What do you think?" he asked Devriess. "One more time?" He bent his knees, took a deep breath, and then put the dry cigarette butt between his lips.

And abruptly the light went dim and gray, and cold rain stung his face, and in his involuntary gasp the smells of diesel exhaust and chocolate were blended on the gusty breeze.

He shuffled to get his footing on the wet cement of the tilted sidewalk, spitting out the instantly-soaked cigarette butt, and though he hugged the newspaper-wrapped bundle to his chest, the oddly narrowed grip of the revolver slipped out of his hand; the gun splashed into the overflowing gutter.

He would instinctively have crouched to retrieve it, but he had to step out of the way of a woman in a white raincoat walking a dog on a leash. A car hissed past beyond the curb, and through its partly-rolled-down window he heard a familiar melody, and of course it was "How Little We Know."

Blanzac squinted through the rain at the other side of the street, and after a few seconds of blinking water out of his eyes he saw a slim figure hurrying east along the sidewalk over there, and then his heart was pounding, for he had recognized her even before he made out the dark hair and blue sweater and black Capri pants.

"Sophie!" he yelled over the wind and the thrashing of the rain. "I love you!"

He knew she hadn't been able to make out his words, but she peered across the lanes in his direction. He waved and slipped on the wet pavement and scrambled to catch his balance, nearly losing the newspaper-wrapped bundle.

Then a darkly-gleaming Buick had pulled to the curb on her side of the street, and a man got out quickly and grabbed her arms; the two figures rocked as she struggled. The woman in the raincoat was shouting something, and the dog was barking; Blanzac unthinkingly took a step out onto the street, letting go of the bundled papers—but a moment later there were *two* men beside the Buick across the street, apparently fighting, and then the first man got hastily back into the car, which sped away to the west.

The newcomer was now walking quickly away to the east with Sophia Greenwald, toward Hyde Street.

A close, loud car-horn made Blanzac jump back onto the curb, and this time he did lose his footing, and he sat down on the wet sidewalk as a taxi hissed past a yard beyond his shoes.

He got back to his feet, rubbing his chilled and abraded palms on his jacket, and he saw that the taxi had run over the bundle—the newspaper was torn and already soaked, and the handwritten pages were fanned out across the asphalt, rapidly darkening with moisture.

Stepping back from the curb, he watched as the tires of two more cars slashed over the papers, scattering them in wet pieces.

He looked up, but Greenwald and her companion had already turned down Hyde Street.

I believe you have some Irish coffee now, he thought, and, even in the moment he thought it, he was blinking in the relatively bright radiance of the overhead light in his office, and both Welch and Devriess were staring at him.

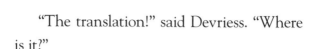

"The translation!" said Devriess. "Where is it?"

"He's dropped the gun," said Welch. "Grab him now!"

"Don't be absurd," said Devriess. He looked more closely at Blanzac, whose hair was now wetly plastered down. "That same day?"

Blanzac nodded. "I threw it in the street. Cars ran over it."

Welch had got to his feet, bracing himself on the desk. "What?" he asked plaintively. "Did I pass out?"

"Get to a hospital," Blanzac told him.

"But—" He looked at the desk and the floor. "Where's the Greenwald translation?"

"Destroyed," said Devriess, hiking his walker forward. "Long ago."

"What the hell are you—it was right here a second ago—wasn't it?"

"I will explain," said Devriess, "in the car."

Welch gave Blanzac a wide-eyed look. "I'll kill you for this." It wasn't clear whether he meant his maimed hand or the lost translation. Probably both, Blanzac thought.

"You don't want that sin too," said Devriess, reaching out to turn the injured man toward the door. To Blanzac he said, "We don't hold this against you. We don't hold anything."

VIII

WHEN THE TAILLIGHTS of their car
had disappeared around the nearest corner,
Blanzac locked the front and kitchen doors
and trudged back up the hall to his office,
and then just stood in the doorway and
looked around.

At his feet the carpet pattern was
obscured by the wide dark patch of Welch's
blood; a yard farther it was missing a broad
oval section over concave floorboards with

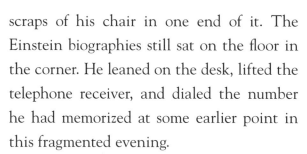

scraps of his chair in one end of it. The Einstein biographies still sat on the floor in the corner. He leaned on the desk, lifted the telephone receiver, and dialed the number he had memorized at some earlier point in this fragmented evening.

After two rings a man answered with an impatient, "Yes?"

"Uh, could I talk to...Betty Barlow, please?"

"Not now. Who is this?"

"My name's Richard Blanzac, I visited her about—"

"Blanzac! One moment."

A woman's voice now said, "Mr. Blanzac? yes, you visited Miss Barlow an hour ago. We were going to call you shortly, since you were the last one to speak with her. Was there anything...did she seem well?"

"Yes," he said; and to test his sudden fearful suspicion, he said, "I'm a book dealer, and she asked me to hold some books for her, awaiting payment."

"I'm afraid she…I'm afraid you can consider the order cancelled."

"She died?"

"She—*was* eighty-six."

Blanzac thanked her and hung up.

She was eighty-six, but in some direction, like a figure seen through the wrong end of a telescope, she was still thirty-one, running down the rainy slope of Hyde Street with him toward the Buena Vista Café.

He picked up another cigarette butt out of the box that had once long ago held jars of pickled garlic, and put it in his mouth, and closed his eyes.

But the air remained still and warm, and when he opened his eyes he was still leaning against his desk in the office.

The discontinuity circuit was apparently closed now; or rather, it had always been closed and would always be there, but he had now irrevocably moved past it in time. And he wondered if, by some law of conservation of reality, the Akan text always necessarily destroyed itself, beause it was a doorway to the god who had destroyed itself.

He put the cigarette butt back in the box, and stood up and stretched, then crossed to the bookcase and reached up into the gap where the Einstein biographies had been, and pulled out the Ace Double.

He crossed back to the desk, pushed the box out of the way and sat down.

Read what I wrote, she had said to him as he'd disappeared from her apartment for the first time—the last time she was ever to see him, until his visit to Goldengrove today. And earlier in that long-ago day she had written something in the book, in the middle pages.

He riffled through it until the pages of *Seconds of Arc* became the upside-down pages of *What Vast Image,* and he had glimpsed ink writing. He flipped back through the pages and found the end of *Seconds of Arc,* right next to a page listing Ace Science Fiction Novels; Greenwald's novel ended halfway down the left-hand page, and below it she had scrawled, *I hope you love me—Sophie.*

The fifty-five-year-old ball-point ink lines had blurred slightly in the yellowed pulp paper.

"And I hope you loved me," he said to the empty room.

He turned to the first page and began to read.